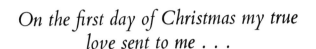

On the first day of Christmas my true
love sent to me . . .

All the world knows the fervent generosity with
which "my true Love" dispatched a succession of
elaborate gifts on the Twelve Days of Christmas.
Yet it has been left to an eleven-year-old authoress
to ponder the recipient's reactions. Here now in
twelve brief Letters of Thanks Manghanita
Kempadoo provides us with a vivid and witty insight
into the lady's hitherto unconsidered predicament.

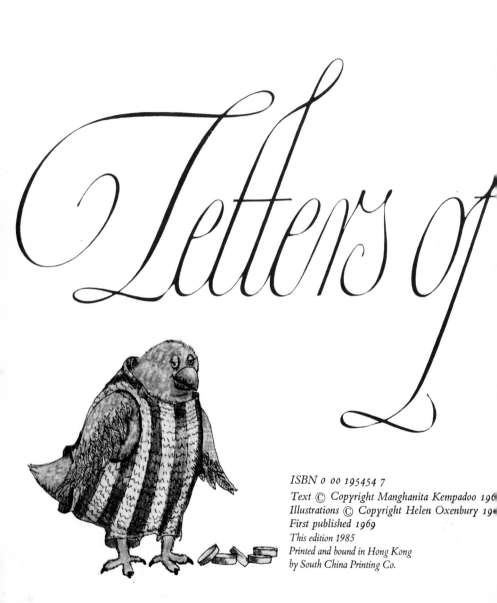

Letters of

ISBN 0 00 195454 7

Text © Copyright Manghanita Kempadoo 196█
Illustrations © Copyright Helen Oxenbury 19█
First published 1969
This edition 1985
Printed and bound in Hong Kong
by South China Printing Co.

Thanks

by Manghanita Kempadoo

illustrated by Helen Oxenbury

Collins

Huntington Hall
December 25th, 1895.

Dear Lord Gilbert,

How delighted I was to receive that dear little partridge in the pear tree. Whenever I look at him I shall remember you, but he does look rather lonely and cold. Maybe he would be better off with a muffler!

Oh, thank you so much for such a thoughtful gift.

Yours lovingly,

Katherine Huntington.

Huntington Hall

December 26th, 1895.

Dear Lord Gilbert,

The two turtle doves arrived safely and are cooing in the pear tree with the partridge.

My head gardener is building a new dove cote as the old one is not quite suitable for them.

The partridge still looks lonely, though I cannot think why!

Yours thankfully,

Katherine Huntington.

Huntington Hall
December 27th, 1895.

Dear Lord Gilbert,

How enchanting the three French hens are!
Do they really come from France? The turtle doves
are quite happy in their dove cote and I think
I will put the French hens with them.

My dear little partridge looks even more
unhappy and I cannot think what to do.

Gratefully yours,

Katherine Huntington.

Huntington Hall
December 28th, 1895.

Dear Lord Gilbert,

How did you know I would like four calling birds. They simply delight me with their singing, although they can be rather noisy.

They are quite friendly with my darling partridge so I cannot imagine why he looks so sad.

The French hens and the turtle doves are cooing in the dove cote. I wonder if I can introduce them to the calling birds?

Yours,

Katherine Huntington.

Dear Lord Gilbert,

Oh, I cannot express my thanks for those lovely golden rings. I cannot possibly think how you knew the sizes. They fit perfectly! They will match my new satin dress that I will wear tonight to Lady Wentwort's ball. This evening I will wear my sapphire chain to match the rings. I simply cannot stop looking at them. You are so thoughtful. My little partridge is shivering with cold. I think I'll make him a woollen suit. Thank you many times over. Yours for ever,

Katherine Huntington.

Huntington Hall
December 30th, 1895.

Dear Lord Gilbert,

Thank you for your unusual gift of six laying geese. My big problem is where to put them. They are, at the moment, ruining my new croquet lawn and hissing. Can you tell me what to do with their eggs? No one seems to want to buy them. I dare not keep them for six geese are quite enough. The partridge is now warm in his new black and yellow woollen suit

Sincerely yours,

Katherine Huntington.

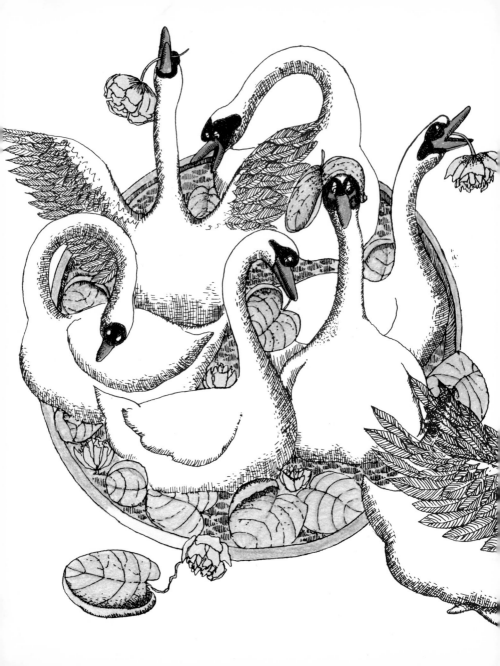

Huntington Hall
December 31st, 1895.

Dear Lord Gilbert,

We had to put the seven swans in my lily pond. They are a bit cramped there, but my lily pond is an absolute _wreck_. Also I do not know what to feed them on.

I think my partridge is afraid of them and that just will not do.

Lady Katherine Huntington.

Huntington Hall

January 1st, 1896

Lord Gilbert,

Eight cows give so much milk that soon we shall have to put the swans to swim in it. The cows made such a noise last night that I could hardly sleep. I also now have to pay eight milking maids. My partridge has a cold from drinking so much milk.

Lady Huntington.

Huntington Hall
January 2nd, 1896.

Lord Gilbert,

One of the nine fiddlers seems to be out of tune. What with their scraping, the cows mooing, pails clanking, honking, hissing and cooing, I have a slight headache. My partridge does not like it at all.

Lady Huntington.

Huntington Hall
Jan. 3rd, 1896.

Lord G. Faraday,
  Your gift of ~~a~~ ten drummers is quite unwelcome.
  They are making me mad.

  Lady K. Huntington.

Huntington Hall, 4.1.96

Lord Faraday,

The eleven ladies dancing are quite outrageous. They make me quite ill

Hon. Lady Huntington

Huntington Hall

5th January 1896

Dear Lord Faraday,

    Lady Katherine has retired to her
London home with the partridge.
She is suffering from a nervous
breakdown.

She requested me to return these
gifts to you:

      Twelve leaping lords

      Eleven dancing ladies

      Ten drummers

      Nine fiddlers

Eight milking maids and their cows

Seven swans

Six laying geese

Four calling birds

Three French hens

Two turtle doves and a pear tree

She wishes to keep the partridge
and rings. *Margaret A.E. Bowes*

Secretary to

Lady Huntington.